The Cowgirl Aunt of
Harriet Bean

Also by Alexander McCall Smith

The Five Lost Aunts of Harriet Bean
Harriet Bean and the League of Cheats
Akimbo and the Elephants
Akimbo and the Lions
Akimbo and the Crocodile Man
Akimbo and the Snakes

Alexander McCall Smith

The Cowgirl Aunt of Harriet Bean

Illustrated by Laura Rankin

BLOOMSBURY
CHILDREN'S
BOOKS

Published by Bloomsbury Publishing, New York, London, and Berlin
Distributed to the trade by Holtzbrinck Publishers

Library of Congress Cataloging-in-Publication Data
McCall Smith, Alexander.
The cowgirl aunt of Harriet Bean / by Alexander McCall Smith ;
illustrations by Laura Rankin.—1st U.S. ed.
p. cm.
Summary: When she joins Aunt Japonica and Aunt Thessalonika on a trip to
America, nine-year-old Harriet meets yet another relative—Aunt Formica, a
cowgirl who is having trouble with some clever and mysterious cattle
rustlers.
ISBN-10: 1-58234-977-0 • ISBN-13: 978-1-58234-977-0
[1. Cowgirls—Fiction. 2. Aunts—Fiction. 3. Robbers and outlaws—Fiction.
4. West (U.S.)—Fiction. 5. Humorous stories.] I. Rankin, Laura, ill.
II. Title.
PZ7.M47833755 Cow 2006   [Fic]—dc22   2006002007

First U.S. Edition 2006

Typeset by Westchester Book Composition
Printed in Mexico

2 4 6 8 10 9 7 5 3 1

Bloomsbury Publishing, Children's Books, U.S.A.
175 Fifth Avenue, New York, NY 10010

For Alison Lyburn

Contents

An Invitation Arrives

I like getting letters from my aunts. Every morning, while my father is still having his breakfast, I go into the hall and check to see what the mailman brought. Often it's dull, very dull—bills in brown envelopes or letters to my father about one of his inventions—but sometimes I see an envelope that lifts my spirits instantly. These are the letters from my aunts.

I have five aunts, you see. You may have read all about them before and, if you have, you'll know all about how they were lost (which was my father's fault) and then found again. And what marvelous aunts they turned out to be! There is Aunt Veronica, the strong lady at the circus; Aunt Harmonica, the ventriloquist; Aunt Majolica, the bossy one (who really isn't so bad after all); and finally Aunts Thessalonika and Japonica, the private detectives and mind readers. Is that all of them? Let me see: Veronica, Harmonica, Majolica, Thessalonika, and Japonica. Yes, that makes five.

Just about every week one of my aunts writes to me. Sometimes it's Aunt Veronica, who tells me where her circus is and what's been happening there. These letters are very exciting. A few weeks ago, she wrote that one of the trapeze artists had fallen off the trapeze while swinging to and fro at the very top of the tent. Fortunately for him, he landed right in the middle of a trampoline that had been set up for the next act, and he bounced right back up to the trapeze again, the right way up. So it all had a happy ending.

Sometimes I get a letter from Aunt Harmonica, who gives me all the news from the opera house, where she is the official voice-thrower. Her last letter was very funny.

"We've just had a terrible emergency," she said. "Halfway through a piece of music, the man who plays the tuba in the orchestra got a terrible attack of hiccups. You can imagine what it sounds like if you hiccup while you're trying to play a great big instrument like the tuba. He couldn't go on. So I had to crawl down into the orchestra pit in front of the stage and make a sound like a tuba for the rest of the piece. It wasn't easy, but I did it, and I don't think anybody in the audience realized what was going on!"

But the letters I most like getting are from my Aunt Thessalonika and Aunt Japonica. They write their letters together, and you never know which words have been written by which aunt! The only time you can tell is when they use different colored pens. It's very easy then.

Their letters are full of the details of their latest case and can make quite scary reading. They often get into all kinds of trouble, but they always seem to get out of it at the end. Last week they had to hide under the bed of a very dangerous criminal when he suddenly returned home while they were searching his house for jewels he had stolen.

"When we heard him at the door," wrote Aunt Thessalonika, "we had to find somewhere to hide. And the only place was right under his bed! So we slid under it and lay there, hoping that he'd go out again soon.

"Unfortunately, he did not go out. Instead, he came straight into the bedroom, changed into his pajamas, and went to bed! You can imagine how we felt. He was quite heavy, and the bed sagged, squashing us. At one point, your Aunt Japonica wanted to sneeze, and was only prevented from doing this by your Aunt Thessalonika holding firmly onto her nose.

"At last we heard snoring from above, and we started to crawl out. I'm sorry to say, though, that we found ourselves stuck, and the only way we could get out of the house was to make our way out with the bed still on top of us. So we did that, on our hands and knees, with the bed on our backs. And that is how we were when we met the policeman in the street outside.

"At first he accused us of stealing the bed, but when he saw who was tucked up inside it, still fast asleep, he changed his mind.

" 'We've been looking for him for a long time!' he exclaimed. 'Thank you very much!'

"So we carried the bed all the way down to the police station—with a little bit of help from the policeman, of course—and set it down there.

"You can imagine the surprise the jewel thief had when he woke up and saw where he was. He was not pleased!"

There had been many other letters like that, and I could hardly wait to see my two detective aunts again. We had had so much fun solving the mystery of the League of Cheats together, and I hoped they would soon invite me to help them out with another one of their cases.

I had a long wait, but at last it came. It

arrived one Saturday morning, a letter from Aunt Thessalonika and Aunt Japonica, inviting me to come with them on what they called a "little trip."

"We are going to America," they wrote. "Would you like to come? That is, of course, if you are free and have nothing better to do."

I could hardly contain my excitement, and I showed the letter to my father. As usual, he hardly paid it any attention, as his mind was on one of his ridiculous inventions. He was trying to invent a portable bath for people who go camping. It was a very strange invention. You got into something that looked like a large waterproof sack. Then you zipped it all the way up to your neck, connected it to a tap with a hose, and turned the water on. After that, you jumped up and down and the water went all over you. There was a plug down at the bottom.

When I showed him the letter, he was testing the plug, which did not seem to be working very well.

"A letter from those aunts of yours?" he

said absentmindedly. "Asking you to go on a little trip? How nice. Well, of course you must go."

"It's all the way to America," I explained, worried that he would object to my going so far.

"America?" he said. "Would you be able to get something for me there? You see, I need a special kind of plug. It's bigger than this one, and it has an odd, slidy bit right here. They make them only in America. Could you pick one up for me?"

I was delighted, and I promised to get the plug. I wrote back to my aunts immediately and said that I would love to go with them to America and that my father had agreed to take me to the airport the following Saturday, which just happened to be the beginning of school vacation.

My aunts wrote back the next day.

"We'll see you at the airport," they said. "But you may not see us. Don't worry, though. We'll send you your ticket and you can just get on the plane. We'll see you sooner or later."

"Sounds very odd," said my father when he read the letter. "But those two aunts of yours have always been a bit strange, if you ask me. I'm not so sure if going off to America is such a good idea after all."

"But what about the plug?" I said quickly.

"Ah yes," he said. "The plug. Well, perhaps it's not such a bad idea after all, but please be careful. Those two aunts get into all kinds of trouble, so keep a close eye on them."

"I will," I promised. "Don't you worry about that!"

A Very Peculiar Trip

I found myself counting the days until it was time to leave for America. Time dragged by slowly, but at last the day of departure came and there I was, my suitcase in my hand, standing in front of the airline desk. My father said good-bye and left me with one of the airline staff. She took my ticket and showed me where I could wait until it was time for the plane to leave.

I looked around the waiting room. There seemed to be hundreds of people milling around, all waiting to get on the plane. I expected to see my aunts, but there was no sign of them. Perhaps they would be the last to arrive and would board the plane just before the doors were closed.

After an hour or so, I still had not seen my aunts, and by now it was time for everybody to get on board. I was starting to get nervous, but I remembered what they had said in the letter and decided that I should do as they told me.

We all got on the plane and found our seats. It was a very full flight, and every seat seemed to be taken. Yet still there was no sign of my aunts. By now I was beginning to think that they had missed the plane after all. Perhaps their bus had broken down on the way to the airport, or perhaps they had even gotten on the wrong plane. I had heard of that happening before. People got on the wrong plane and ended up in the wrong corner of the world. Then a terrible thought came to me: perhaps I was on the wrong plane myself! Perhaps I would find myself in Bombay or Buenos Aires, or even Bulawayo! What would I do then?

It was too late. The doors of the plane had been slammed shut and the big engines started. Slowly we taxied out onto the runway, and then with a throaty roar the plane set off on its journey. Within seconds, we were in the air and headed up into the clouds. We were on our way.

Once we were airborne, I decided that I should stop worrying and enjoy the trip. I sat back in my seat and looked out the window. I was admiring the view, thinking how nice it would be to bounce up and down on top of the clouds below us, when there was a tap on my shoulder.

I looked around to see one of the stewardesses smiling at me.

"Would you like some orange juice?" she asked. "Or perhaps something to eat?"

I asked for orange juice, and the stewardess smiled and went off to get it. As she did so, a very strange feeling came over me. I had seen that stewardess before somewhere;

I was sure of it. But I had never been on a plane before, and so I wondered how I could possibly know her.

I was thinking about this, feeling very puzzled, when the stewardess came back and handed me a large cup of orange juice.

"I hope you enjoy that, Harriet," she said.

"Thank you," I said. "I'm sure I will . . ."

I stopped. She had called me Harriet. Yet how could she possibly know who I was?

I was about to ask, but she had already turned her back to me and was busy taking care of another passenger. I would have to wait and ask her when she walked past me again. I could find out her name and ask her where we had met before.

A few minutes later she came by.

"Excuse me," I said, reaching out to touch the sleeve of her jacket. "Could you tell me—"

I did not have time to finish my question. The stewardess had turned to me and bent down to whisper in my ear.

"Can't you see?" she whispered. "I'm your aunt Thessalonika!"

I was speechless. I looked at her closely and realized that it was true. Aunt Thessalonika was very well disguised, but it was clearly her. No wonder I had thought we had seen each other before! Of course I was relieved that I was not alone on the plane after all, but at the same time I wondered what on earth she was doing disguised as a stewardess. And where was Aunt Japonica? Was she disguised as one of the other passengers? Was that fat man sitting in the row in front of me really an aunt with a pillow stuffed into her pants? Nothing would surprise me with these aunts.

My question was soon answered—or almost answered. Several minutes later, walking down the aisle of the plane in a smart blue uniform, his cap under his arm, greeting the passengers, came the captain of the plane. Or was it? As he walked past my row of seats, he paused and smiled in my direction.

I looked up, unsure what to do. There was something familiar about him, although I couldn't decide what it was. Was it something in his eyes? Or something in the way he walked? It was difficult to tell, but I had a very strong suspicion that the captain was none other than my aunt Japonica, heavily disguised of course, but nonetheless my aunt!

I must admit that I felt a little bit worried for the rest of the flight. I knew that my aunts were extraordinarily good at disguises, and I knew that there was nobody better at mind reading than they were. But flying a plane was a very special job, and even Aunt Japonica might find it a bit difficult.

I did not have the chance to ask. Aunt Thessalonika was far too busy looking after the passengers to talk to me, and I never saw the captain again. But we landed safely, I'm happy to say, and soon I found myself getting off the plane in New York and stepping for the first time onto American soil.

I collected my suitcase and waited at the exit. I did not have long to wait, as down the corridor came my two aunts, dressed as themselves and chatting excitedly.

"Were you . . . ," I began to ask Aunt

Japonica. "I mean, did you really fly the plane?"

Aunt Japonica looked surprised.

"Fly a plane? My goodness me, Harriet! I don't think I could do that!"

"But where were you?" I asked.

My aunts looked at each other and smiled.

"Later on, Harriet," they said. "We'll discuss all that later on. The important thing is that we've arrived in America and there are lots and lots of exciting things for us to do!"

A Very Surprising Story

I was very excited by America. Everything around me seemed so big and bright, and everybody, everywhere, seemed to be in such a rush. We rushed too, driving in a long yellow taxi to a hotel that my aunts had chosen in advance. Then, in the hotel, we stepped into an elevator and went shooting up to the thirty-ninth floor.

There was a marvelous view from the window of our room. In every direction, as far as the eye could see, there stretched the great city. Tall buildings stuck up like giant pencils, and way down below us in the street, we could make out tiny cars and minute, antlike people.

I was very tired from the long flight and so I went to bed almost right away. But just before I did, a waiter brought up a tray with a hamburger, a bowl of banana ice cream, and a large tub of popcorn.

"Junk food!" he called out cheerfully. "A whole delicious trayful!"

I eagerly ate my first meal in America and then, feeling perfectly contented, drifted off to sleep.

The next morning, Aunt Japonica and Aunt Thessalonika took me down to breakfast on the fifteenth floor.

"We must move on today," said Aunt Japonica. "We've got a lot to do in America."

"You're right," agreed Aunt Thessalonika. "There's no time to lose."

I was not sure what it was that we were supposed to be doing. My aunts had told me nothing about why they had come to America. The reason was bound to be exciting, though. Nothing in their lives was the slightest bit dull.

"Where are we going?" I asked. I really liked New York—what I had seen of it—and I wasn't sure that I wanted to move on.

"West," Aunt Japonica said simply. "We're going west."

That sounded intriguing, but I still wasn't sure what we were going to do.

"Why are we going west?" I asked. "Do you have a case out there?"

Both aunts looked at me in a very surprised way.

"But surely you know why we're here, Harriet?" Aunt Japonica said. "Didn't we tell you about your aunt Formica?"

For a moment I was too astonished to say anything at all. Aunt Formica? Did I have yet another aunt? I thought that I had found them all by now, but here we were going off to see somebody called Aunt Formica. It was all very puzzling.

Aunt Japonica stared at me a few seconds longer and then shook her head.

"It's all your father's fault," she said with a sigh. "He never seems to tell you anything."

"Yes," said Aunt Thessalonika. "To think that poor Harriet never heard of Formica. It really is too bad!"

"Then please tell me," I urged. "I'd really like to hear all about her."

Aunt Japonica looked at her watch.

"Not now," she said. "We have a train to catch. But once we're on the train there'll be plenty of time for us to tell you all about your aunt Formica."

And there was. As our train made its way across the wide plains of America, Aunt Japonica told me all about my sixth lost aunt, and what had happened to her.

"You'll remember," she said, "how the family had to split up after the farm was sold all those years ago? Well, after we had all gone to our different homes, our father and mother had another baby. But because the family had split up by then, we never heard about her. So for a long time we didn't even know that we had a younger sister."

"That's right," said Aunt Thessalonika.

"And so it came as a great surprise to all of us when one Christmas we received a card signed, quite simply, 'Your sister Formica.' "

Aunt Japonica nodded. "Of course we were very excited about it, and we all wrote letters to her to find out who she was and where she lived. I wrote first, I think, and I had a long letter back. She told me that shortly after she was born, our parents became poorer and found it difficult to buy food even for their new baby. Fortunately, there was a cousin in America, and she offered to take in the baby and look after her there. And that is how Formica got here."

It all seemed very strange and exciting to me, but by now I was becoming used to the extraordinary lives that all my aunts had led.

"She traveled all the way to America by herself," Aunt Japonica went on. "Can you imagine that? She was only two at the time, but she was very, very brave, and people on the ship were very kind to her.

"Then, when she reached the other side of the Atlantic, she was taken all the way to the west and brought up on a ranch. She learned to ride horses, lasso cattle with a long rope, and cook beans over a campfire out on the range. In other words—"

"She became a cowgirl," interjected Aunt Thessalonika. "Just like a cowboy, but a girl."

I sat with my mouth wide open in astonishment. The story of Aunt Formica was far more exciting than I ever could have imagined, and I was thrilled at the thought that I had a cowgirl aunt. I imagined her riding up to meet us on her horse, throwing her hat into the air, and firing pistol shots through it. It was all very exciting.

"She was very good at being a cowgirl," said Aunt Japonica. "When her cousin became too old to run the ranch, she gave it to Formica, and Formica has looked after it since then. She went to rodeos and won all the prizes for breaking in horses and riding on the backs of great fierce bulls."

"But then it all went wrong," said Aunt Thessalonika. "Something happened to spoil it."

"What was that?" I blurted out.

My aunts shrugged. "We don't know," said Aunt Japonica. "All we know is that she wrote to us and asked us to come out as soon as we possibly could. Something was going dreadfully wrong, but she didn't say what it was."

"So we're going to help her," I said. "And that's why we're heading west."

"Yes," said Aunt Japonica, adding glumly, "I only hope it's not too late. I've got a terrible feeling that it might be."

I felt very worried. Whatever was happening did sound very bad, and I hoped that our train would hurry up and complete its journey so that we could see what we could do to help.

Home on the Range . . .

The train journey seemed to take forever. We had bunks to sleep in, and everything was very comfortable, but I was itching to arrive. At last, though, just when I thought that we would never get there, my aunts consulted their map and told me to get my things ready to get off the train.

"That last stop was Cactus Point," said Aunt Japonica. "According to this map, the next stop is ours."

I asked what it was called and Aunt Japonica looked at her map again.

"Skeleton Gulch," she said in a slightly disapproving tone. "Towns can have very strange names in America." She looked at the map again and shook her head. "I see that there's a place here called Poison. Can you imagine that?"

Poison sounded pretty bad, I had to admit, but what about Skeleton Gulch? That was almost as unwelcoming.

I looked out the window of the train. The wheat fields through which we had been traveling had given way to hills and valleys, and everything was a bit drier. It was hotter, too, with a great burning sun overhead and no clouds in the wide blue sky. So this was the West!

Skeleton Gulch was not much of a place. We saw it all as the train drew into the station. There was the station building, which was not much more than a low shack, a water tower, and a street of rickety-looking wooden buildings. If you've ever seen a cowgirl film, you'll know just what it looked like.

We were the only people to get off the train. The conductor, who had been very friendly to us on the journey, helped us unload our luggage.

"I don't know what you're doing getting off in a place like this," he said, frowning. "I can't remember when anybody last got off here."

I looked around. There was nobody around, as far as I could see. Skeleton Gulch seemed to be utterly deserted. Perhaps it's a ghost town, I thought. I had read about these places. They were towns where nobody lived at all. Everybody had gone away, and nobody else had come in their place. So all the houses were left exactly where they were, with nobody to live in them except the rats and the snakes.

My thoughts were interrupted by Aunt Japonica.

"This way, Harriet," she said sharply. "It's far too hot to stand around thinking about ghost towns."

It's strange having aunts who are mind readers. They can tell what you're thinking almost all the time. You have to be careful what you think, too. You can't think thoughts like, I wish my aunt wouldn't wear that terrible hat; or, I'm bored and I wish my aunt would stop talking. They can tell when you're thinking things like that and they look at you in a very disapproving way.

I picked up my suitcase and followed my aunts. Since there was nobody in the station, we had nobody to take our tickets. So we just walked out onto the street and looked around.

"We'll have to ask the way," said Aunt Thessalonika. "I hope it's not too far."

But how could we ask the way, I wondered, when there was nobody around to ask? I was beginning to feel frightened. Why was Skeleton Gulch called Skeleton Gulch?

Just as I was thinking this, we heard a loud creaking noise. It made me jump, and I spun around to see the door in one of the wooden buildings open and a man step out. He looked at us, rubbed his eyes, and then gave a friendly wave.

"Did you folks get off the train?" he called out.

"We did," said Aunt Japonica.

"Well, well," said the man, coming over to meet us. "That's the most unusual thing that's happened 'round these parts for well on . . . six months. Yes, that's right. Nobody's gotten off that train for six months. Normally that old train just whistles right through here."

"We're looking for our sister," explained Aunt Thessalonika. "She's called Formica, and we believe she lives around here."

The man smiled. "She certainly does," he said. "She lives up Rattlesnake Creek way. And I'll take you there in my truck if you like, because I'm the local taxi driver and that's my job!"

We were very pleased to have met the taxi driver, and when he came back a few minutes later with his old brown truck, we loaded in our luggage and set off with him. It was a bumpy ride. The roads were full of holes and here and there we had to swerve to avoid a branch that had fallen from a tree. But before too long we were bouncing along a farm road and there, set between two small hills, with a wide plain behind it, was Aunt Formica's ranch house.

"This is it," said the taxi driver as we drew to a halt in a cloud of dust. "This is Formica's place."

We thanked him, lifted out our suitcases, and waved as he drove away. Then we turned around and looked at the house. The front door was open, but there was no sign of anybody around. So we sat down on the porch in front of the house and waited for something to happen.

Suddenly it did. From behind the house there came a great whooping noise and the sound of galloping hooves. Then, before we even had time to stand up and see what it was, there was a cloud of dust, and a shout, and a horse came to a stop right in front of the porch.

"Whoa!" shouted the rider as she jumped off the horse, landing perfectly on the high heels of her tall cowgirl boots.

"Formica!" shouted Aunt Japonica and Aunt Thessalonika in unison.

"Japonica!" shouted the rider. "Thessalonika!"

My two aunts tumbled down the steps to hug their sister. Then they turned around and pointed at me. Aunt Formica walked toward me and shook me by the hand. Her hand felt strong and rough, and I liked her the moment I saw her. So this was my sixth aunt! I could hardly believe my luck. This wonderful rider, with her wide-brimmed hat and her silver jingling spurs, was my aunt. It was almost too good to be true.

Aunt Formica took us into the house and showed us to our rooms. Then we all went into the kitchen and sat on stools while she prepared supper. We had beans, of course, which is what cowgirls always eat, and they tasted marvelous, cooked on her small wood-burning stove. Then we drank coffee out of tin mugs. I don't normally like coffee, but the way Aunt Formica made it was just right, and it went very well with the beans.

As we ate, Aunt Formica explained why

she had asked her two sisters to come out and help her.

"I knew that you two were just the people to sort all of this out," she said. "And with Harriet to help you, I'm sure that we'll get to the bottom of it in no time at all."

"But what is *it*?" pressed Aunt Japonica. "None of us has the slightest idea what your problem really is."

It was just beginning to get dark outside, and Aunt Formica lowered her voice, as if there were people out in the darkness who might hear.

"Rustling," she said. "I've got rustlers!"

I wasn't at all sure what rustling was, but what Aunt Formica said next made it all clear.

"Rustlers are the worst thing that can happen to a rancher," she went on to say. "They come at night and take your cattle. They drive them away from under your very nose, and the next morning they're gone. Several of the ranchers near here have been driven out of business by them. They've had to leave

their ranches and go live in Skeleton Gulch—
and that's no fun, as you can imagine."

Aunt Japonica and Aunt Thessalonika
bristled with anger.

"But surely you can get them stopped,"
said Aunt Thessalonika. "What about the
sheriff? Surely you have a sheriff to look out
for you?"

Aunt Formica let out a snort of laughter.
"Sheriff? Yes, we've got a sheriff, all right.
But he's a real clod-hopping, coyote-
baiting . . . he's as much use as a hole in the
head. He hasn't arrested anybody for at least
ten years, and most of the time he sits in
front of his office fast asleep. He's hopeless.
He's worse than hopeless!"

My aunts were silent for a few moments.

"These rustlers are just thieves, aren't
they?" said Aunt Japonica. "They're nothing
but cowardly thieves who steal other people's cattle by night. If only I could get my
hands on them!"

"That's just what I feel too," said Aunt
Formica. "But the trouble is that nobody

ever sees them. They come by night and they leave no tracks. Nobody knows who they are or where they live. All we know is that we're losing our cattle."

I felt just as angry as my aunts. But at the same time, I knew that if there was anybody who could solve the mystery and deal with the rustlers, it would be my two detective aunts.

"Don't worry," I said to Aunt Formica. "Aunt Japonica and Aunt Thessalonika can deal with this for you. If I were a rustler now, I'd be very, very worried."

Aunt Formica looked doubtful. "I hope you're right, Harriet," she said. "But these people must be very clever and very dangerous. I'm afraid it won't be easy."

Aunt Japonica rubbed her hands. "Harriet's right, Formica," she said. "We've dealt with people like this before. We'll find them for you and then you can teach them a lesson or two. But we'll have to start tomorrow, because we're all feeling tired after the journey and I think it's time for bed."

I lay awake that night, watching from my bed as the moon moved slowly across the night sky outside. From time to time I heard a coyote howl, a long wail that echoed up to the stars and back. Were there cattle rustlers out tonight, riding quietly through the darkness, wearing black handkerchiefs over their faces? I was sure that there were, and I felt that tomorrow, when we went to look at the cattle with Aunt Formica, we would find that the thieves had struck again. I shivered at the thought, and snuggled down into my bed until at last I fell asleep.

Rustlers at Work

Aunt Formica woke me early in the morning.

"I've brought you some new clothes," she said, laying them out on the end of the bed. "These are some of the things that I used to wear when I was a girl. They're still in good condition though, and you can try them on. If you're going to be a cowgirl, you must wear the right things."

I tried on the new clothes eagerly. They fit me exactly, and they were very nice as well. There was a pair of riding pants with leather trim, a jacket with fringe around the top, and a plaid shirt with lots of pockets. What I liked most, though, were the boots. These were made of beautiful leather, with a picture of a horse engraved on each of them, and with splendid silver buckles at the ankles.

I felt very proud of my new outfit, and when I went to join my aunts for breakfast, I was delighted to see that both Aunt Japonica and Aunt Thessalonika were now dressed in exactly the same style as I was.

We ate our beans and drank our coffee and then went out to saddle our horses. My horse had white and brown patches and was called Tex. He seemed pleased to see me and was very happy when I gave him a sugar lump before I put on his saddle.

Once we were all mounted, Aunt Formica tossed her hat in the air, caught it deftly, and gave a loud whoop. Then off we rode, with Aunt Formica leading the way. I am not a very good rider, but Tex was a very easy horse to ride. He was also very kind. If I bumped up into the air, he would give a glance up to ensure that he was exactly below me when I came down again. It would be very difficult, if not impossible, to fall off a horse like that.

We rode for half an hour or so, out onto the range. The land was vast—stretching out in every direction were fields of dry brown grass, hills with rocky outcrops, and the occasional cactus.

Suddenly Aunt Formica gave a shout and signaled for us to stop.

"There they are," she said. "That's the cattle over there."

She pointed to a cluster of small brown shapes in the distance and turned her horse in their direction. We galloped over, the horses jumping over ditches and cactuses, and we soon reached where the cattle were grazing.

Aunt Formica got off her horse and started to count.

"Twenty-four, twenty-five—no, I've already counted that one—twenty-five, twenty-six, twenty-seven!"

When she reached twenty-seven, she took off her hat and wiped her brow. I could see that she was upset.

"They've been here," she said simply.

"Rustlers?" I asked.

"Yes," she sighed. "They've taken ten away. There were thirty-seven cattle here yesterday, and now there are only twenty-seven."

As Aunt Formica spoke, Aunt Japonica dismounted and tied the reins of her horse to a nearby cactus. Then she bent down and began to examine the ground very closely. Aunt Thessalonika joined her, and Aunt Formica and I watched as the two famous detectives got down on their hands and knees and searched for signs of what had happened.

After a while, they got up and brushed the sand from their pant legs.

"These people are cunning," said Aunt Japonica. "They've been careful to leave no tracks."

"But how do they do that?" I asked. "Surely their horses would leave some hoof-prints in the ground?"

Aunt Japonica shook her head. "Not if you're as clever as they are," she said. "Not if you put special hoof covers on your horse, *and not if those hoof covers are the same shape as the cattle hooves!*"

I drew in my breath. If the rustlers were as cunning as this, then they would be very difficult to catch, even by people as clever as my aunts.

"So what do we do now?" asked Aunt Formica. "The ground is covered with cattle tracks here. We can't possibly work out which ones really belong to the rustlers."

Aunt Japonica nodded. "Yes, it will be difficult . . ." She paused, staring down at the ground as if she had seen something particularly important. Then she knelt down again and peered at something in the sand.

"Very interesting," she said. "Formica, do any of your cattle have only three legs?"

Aunt Formica laughed. "What a ridiculous question, Japonica," she said. "No cow has three legs."

"In that case," said Aunt Japonica, "One of the rustlers has been very careless. He has forgotten to put on one of his horse's hoof covers. Look at these odd tracks. Three cattle prints and one horse's hoofprint!"

We all looked down and saw that what

Aunt Japonica said was true. Now at last we had a trail, and if we followed it, we would be able to find out the direction from which the rustlers had come. That at least would be a start.

We got back on our horses, and with Aunt Japonica in the lead this time, staring hard at the ground, we set off. The trail led straight across the plain, toward some hills in the distance, and we followed it for at least an hour. Then we hit some rocky ground, and no matter how hard we searched, the trail had disappeared.

"That's it, I'm afraid," said Aunt Japonica. "I can't follow this any further."

It was disappointing, but at least we knew now that the rustlers had come down from the hills.

"We will have to go back to the ranch now," said Aunt Formica. "If we're going to go up into the hills, we're going to need tents and other supplies. It's not going to be easy going up there."

I was thrilled at the thought of what lay

ahead. This was the Wild West exactly as it should be. We were going up into the hills. We were going to take tents with us. Anything could happen up there, I thought—anything.

Anything Happens

We packed quickly. Aunt Formica divided what we had to carry into four, and we stuffed it all into our saddlebags. Then we were all given hats. Aunt Japonica got a rather tattered old hat, with a tear in the brim—but it looked good on her and she seemed very pleased. Aunt Thessalonika's hat was newer but had a few bullet holes in it, which made her feel a little worried. I was luckiest—my hat was just like Aunt Formica's, a large white one, with the widest brim of all. It was exactly the sort of hat a cowgirl should have, and I felt very brave in it as I walked out to my horse.

Aunt Formica rode in front, and we were soon well on our way to the hills. It was a long ride, though, and we had to rest the horses several times on our way there. But at last, just before lunchtime, we arrived at the first of the rocky outcrops that marked the end of the plain.

We ate our lunch sitting beneath some trees. Afterward, while the horses were still tied up and my aunts were drinking the coffee Aunt Formica had brewed over a small fire, I decided to explore my surroundings a little.

"Don't be long," warned Aunt Formica. "We'll have to get along in half an hour or so. And make sure you're careful of the—"

Just at that moment, one of the horses neighed, and I didn't hear what Aunt Formica said. But I would be careful anyway, I thought. It was probably the sun she wanted me to watch out for, as it was very strong. Well, I had my wide-brimmed hat and that was as good as a sun umbrella, I thought.

I clambered over some rocks that lay behind us. There was a small hillock nearby, and I thought that if I climbed it I would be able to get a good view of our surroundings and also wave to my aunts down below.

I began to climb. Everything was very dusty, and I had to be careful of the prickly cactuses that grew between the rocks, but soon I was almost at the top.

I sat down to get my breath back, and looked down below. There were my three aunts, sitting under their tree, chatting away, while the horses dozed in the background.

Suddenly I heard a noise. It was a peculiar noise, like the sound of something being dragged over a rough surface. It was a sort of scratchy sound, I suppose, and at first I didn't pay much attention to it. Instead I looked up into the sky, which was blue and empty, and seemed to stretch out forever and ever.

Then the noise came back. It was louder now, and closer, and in an awful moment I realized what it was. It was a rattling sound, as if dice had been put in a cup and shaken very hard. It was an angry noise, as if something were trying to warn me.

I looked around and immediately saw what it was. There, in front of me, in a little space between two rocks was a large, thick snake, its tail raised behind it, shaking rapidly to and fro. It was a rattlesnake, a big one, and it was staring straight at me, its little eyes burning with anger.

When I saw it, my heart gave a great thump and turned right over. The snake seemed to sense this, and its tail shook even faster, making the rattle sound all the more threatening.

I forced myself to stay still, remembering what I had once read about being faced with a snake. Any sudden movement might disturb it, and force it to strike. You had to remain calm. Now I knew what Aunt Formica had been warning me about. I was supposed to be careful of rattlesnakes. If only I had heard her, I probably wouldn't have climbed up there in the first place. If there's one thing I'm frightened of, it's snakes. And now here I

was with an angry rattlesnake at my feet and no idea at all what to do next.

The snake was still watching me intently. I suppose it was thinking what to do too, wondering whether to bite me now, from a distance, or to get a little closer and get a better bite. I moved my foot a little, hoping to see whether I would be able to stand up and run, but this just made the snake shake its rattle even more loudly, as if to warn me not to try anything so foolish.

I tried closing my eyes. Perhaps it was just a dream, or even a mirage. I knew that in very hot places there are things called mirages, which are caused by the shimmering of the hot air. If you see a mirage, you think you see something which isn't really there. But the snake was there when I opened my eyes again. It was still as large as life, shaking its tail, its tiny black tongue darting in and out of its mouth.

I decided that I would have to do something. If the snake was going to bite me anyway, I might as well try to get away first. It just might work.

I looked around, trying hard not to move my head too sharply. There were a few stones near my right hand, some of them very large. If I picked one of them up, I thought, I could throw it at the snake and drive it away. But what if I missed? That would just make the snake angrier than ever and it would be sure to lunge forward and bite me. If it did that, I knew I would be in serious trouble. Rattlesnakes are deadly poisonous, and even a small bite can make you very ill.

Then I thought again. If only I could attract my aunts' attention, they would be able to help me. I was sure that Aunt Formica knew how to deal with rattlesnakes. Would they hear me if I shouted out? Would the wind carry my voice down to the trees below? I thought it was way too far, but at least I could try. Snakes were deaf, weren't they? Hadn't I read somewhere that snakes relied on vibrations in the ground, rather than sound, to warn them of danger?

I called out, softly at first, but then louder.

"Aunt Formica!" I yelled. "There's a rattlesnake! Help!"

The snake took no notice, but neither did Aunt Formica. All that happened was that my voice, which sounded so small anyway, bounced back at me from the rocks all around. Nobody would ever hear.

Then I had another idea. Aunt Thessalonika and Aunt Japonica! They may not know much about rattlesnakes, but they were, after all, famous mind readers. If I could get a message to them just by thinking it, then they could alert Aunt Formica to my problem.

I looked down in the direction of my aunts. Then I began to think, very clearly: "Help!" I thought. "Help! Help! Help!"

I frowned with the effort, sending my thoughts down to my aunts below, but it seemed to make no difference. All three aunts were still seated underneath the tree, their backs to me.

I thought again.

"Snake!" I thought. Nothing. Then, a brilliant idea: "Rattle! Rattle!" I thought, making a rattling sound in my mind. "Rattle!"

As I did so, I suddenly saw Aunt Japonica stand up in the distance. She turned around, looked up in my direction, and gestured to the other two. They stood up too.

"Rattle!" I thought again. "Rattle!"

It was working! From where I was sitting, I could now see the aunts begin to run up toward me. They're coming to my rescue, I thought, my heart giving a leap of joy. I'll be saved after all!

The snake was watching me closely. It must have been getting a little bit bored, because it started to move toward me, ever so slowly, stopping from time to time to give its rattle a good shake. "Please hurry!" I thought to my aunts. "Please hurry!"

Suddenly, I heard a shout.

"Stay where you are, everybody! Stay very still!"

It was Aunt Formica's voice, and I looked

down and saw Aunt Japonica and Aunt Thessalonika freeze where they were. Everybody had seen the snake now, and I could see the expression of horror on Aunt Japonica's face.

Aunt Formica moved forward slowly. The snake had not seen her yet, although she was now close to it, approaching from behind.

Suddenly the snake whipped around, its tail shaking like the pendulum of a clock that had gone out of control.

It was now facing Aunt Formica, who stood only a short distance away from it. I looked on in horror. Surely it would bite her now—it was well within striking distance.

What happened next occurred so quickly that I almost didn't see it. Aunt Formica seemed to jump forward, as if she were going to pounce on the snake, but twisted as she did so. At the same time, her hand shot out and there was a little cloud of dust.

For a moment Aunt Formica and the snake seemed to be a twisting, rattling bundle. Then everything settled down and to my utter surprise, Aunt Formica straightened up.

There, on the ground below her, was a bundle of writhing snake, neatly tied in a knot! The rattle was still shaking, but the snake was so confused that the sound was only halfhearted.

"That'll keep him busy for a few hours," laughed Aunt Formica. "He'll be able to untie himself eventually, but it won't be before suppertime!"

I got to my feet, feeling rather shaky.

"We heard you rattling," said Aunt Japonica as she stepped forward to check that I was all right.

"I knew you would," I said. "And thank you very much."

As I spoke, I thought how lucky I was to have such aunts. Would any other girl, without aunts like that, have gotten out of such trouble in one piece? There was only one answer. She would not have.

The Rustlers' Camp

Feeling very pleased at my escape from danger, I said good-bye to the wriggling snake. It was still trying to work out what had happened, staring at its own rattle and wondering whether to bite it or try to untie it. The effort of all this thinking made the rattle shake in irritation, which made the snake more confused and more cross.

We began to make our way down the hillside, back to where the horses were tethered. Or rather, back to where they *had* been tethered.

"The horses!" shouted Aunt Thessalonika. "Look, they're gone."

"They must have run away," said Aunt Japonica. "Formica, do your horses run away?"

Aunt Formica shook her head grimly. "No," she said. "Never. They're far too loyal for that."

It was left to me to say what everyone else was thinking.

"They've been stolen," I said. "Rustled."

Aunt Formica nodded. "I'm afraid you're right, Harriet," she said. "We've been made fools of. Absolute fools!"

We stood under the trees where we had tied the horses and looked around. There was no sign of what had happened. There was no evidence that the horses had put up a struggle; they must simply have been led off by the rustlers while we were up the hill. It must have been the easiest theft the rustlers had been able to carry out for a long time— even easier than stealing cattle.

I looked down at the ground. There were plenty of tracks this time, and I thought it would be easy for us to follow them.

"They went that way," I said, pointing in

the direction of the tracks. "If we hurry, we should be able to catch up with them."

Aunt Japonica shook her head.

"No, Harriet," she said. "You're quite wrong. When you've been a detective as long as I have, then you'll know that there's one golden rule: nothing is what it seems to be—ever."

"But that's the way the tracks are pointing," I protested. "They must have gone that way."

"No," said Aunt Japonica firmly. "That's what they want us to think. The tracks will go that way for a while and then, when they reach stony ground where the hoofprints won't show, they'll turn around and go in the opposite direction. They think they can fool us that easily!"

Aunt Formica looked a little doubtful, but Aunt Thessalonika quickly supported her sister.

"Japonica's right," she said. "They must have gone that way!"

And with that she pointed in the opposite direction.

I was unsure, but I knew that my detective

aunts were famous for always being right about these things, so I bit my tongue and didn't argue anymore. Off we went, trudging through the heat, thinking how much easier it was to ride rather than walk.

"Just wait until I catch those rustlers," said Aunt Formica grimly. "I'll really fix them!"

I remembered what Aunt Formica had done to the rattlesnake, and thought that I would not like to be in the rustlers' shoes. But at the same time, part of me was a little frightened. After all, rustlers are large, tough men with stubbly beards and big muscles. It might not be as easy to tie *them* up in knots!

We walked for an hour or so before Aunt Formica suddenly gave out a cry of triumph.

"There!" she shouted. "Look! Tracks!"

We all peered down at the ground. Yes, sure enough, there were hoofprints right in front of us, and they were going in exactly the direction predicted by Aunt Japonica.

"Now all we have to do is follow these," said Aunt Japonica. "We can't go wrong."

Aunt Formica was not so sure. "We'll have to be careful," she said. "I think we should go on only a little bit farther and then wait. It will be getting dark before too long, and that will give us our chance."

I shivered. Our chance for what? What would we be doing once it got dark? Nobody had discussed what we would do once we caught up with the rustlers. And what if the rustlers were actually following *us*? Nobody had thought of that yet.

I looked over my shoulder nervously. But all I saw were the dry rocky sides of the valley we had been following and a few scraps of tumbleweed being blown by the wind. And yet somewhere, perhaps hidden up in the rocks, I felt that there were eyes watching—watching our every move.

We stopped just before nightfall. The hoofprints were very clear now, which Aunt Japonica explained meant that the rustlers were only a short ways away. I was happy to stop, as I was tired, and a little bit scared.

"We'll sit here until it's completely dark," said Aunt Formica. "Then we can see what's what."

I sat down next to Aunt Thessalonika and snuggled up to her for comfort.

"Don't worry, Harriet," she said. "We've never come off second best, you know."

I nodded.

"And you've seen what Aunt Formica can do," she went on.

I nodded again. I felt a little bit safer, I suppose, but now that it was dark all the rocks seemed to be menacing dark shapes and everything looked so big and so empty. I looked up at the sky. High above me, field upon field of stars hung in the clear air, tiny dots of white light.

Aunt Formica stood up and tapped me on the shoulder.

"Time to move on," she said. "If we go on just a bit, we should see their campfire."

I rose to my feet and followed Aunt

Thessalonika. Aunt Formica led the way, with Aunt Japonica behind her, and the two of us bringing up the rear.

We crept through the darkness, taking care not to bump into rocks or cactuses as we went. I tried not to imagine all the things that we could tread on. I tried especially hard to avoid thinking of rattlesnakes. It would be easy to step on one, I thought. Even Aunt Formica could be outsmarted by a rattle-snake in the pitch dark.

Suddenly Aunt Formica stopped. "Look!" she whispered. "There it is!"

I peered through the darkness. At first I saw nothing, but then I saw it in the distance, a tiny point of flickering yellow light.

"That's their campfire," said Aunt Formica in a low voice. "Cowboys are often afraid of the dark. Campfires make them feel safer."

I was astonished to hear this. "And cow-girls?" I asked. "Do they make campfires too?"

"Hush," said Aunt Formica. "No, they don't. Cowgirls aren't afraid of the dark, you see."

I felt much better when I heard this. I could imagine the rustlers huddling together around the campfire, glancing over their shoulders, trying not to think what the shadows were.

"Now," went on Aunt Formica, "we can get a good deal closer. But once we get really close, then we'll have to get down on our hands and knees and crawl the last little way. And whatever you do, don't make any noise."

We approached the rustlers' camp very slowly, but at last we were close enough to make them out—all five of them—sitting around the fire, eating their beans. They looked pretty frightening to me. They were all tall, strong men, wearing red plaid shirts and high boots. One of them, who had finished his beans before the others, was strumming on a guitar.

We knelt down behind a bush and looked at the rustlers.

"Galloping gophers!" exclaimed Aunt

Formica. "What nerve they've got! Look! There are our horses."

The rustlers had tied our horses to a nearby tree, along with their own horses. And in the background somewhere, we could hear the cattle moving around in the darkness. We had caught them red-handed with stolen cattle *and* stolen horses!

How Cowgirls Fix Rustlers

I was still not sure what we were going to do. We were miles and miles away from anywhere, and you couldn't just run off and call the sheriff. Besides, as Aunt Formica had pointed out, the sheriff was worse than useless, and I was sure that he would never get out of his bed at night, even to arrest a group of rustlers.

"What now?" I whispered.

Aunt Formica turned to me and smiled. I could see the smile because the flickering light from the fire reflected on her face. She looked as if she were about to have some fun.

"Can you crawl quietly?" she asked me.

I nodded. "I think so."

"Then will you crawl over to my horse and get the rope from its saddlebag?" asked Aunt Formica. "You're smaller than we are, and you're bound to make less noise."

I gulped. The thought of getting that close to the rustlers was scary, and yet I could not refuse to play my part in the plan, whatever the plan was.

"Off you go then," said Aunt Formica. "And good luck!"

I crawled as quietly as I could. But even being as careful as possible, I couldn't help but make some noise. At one point I even knelt on a twig, which broke with a loud snapping sound.

The rustler who was strumming his guitar stopped in the middle of a line of song.

"Those ghost riders in the sk—"

I froze, my heart thumping within me like a giant hammer. But after a moment, he must have decided that it was one of the cows, as he started to sing again.

I continued with my task and eventually reached the horse. Once there, I felt in the saddlebag and took out a large coil of rope. Then I crawled back, greatly relieved, to where my brave and exciting aunts were waiting for me.

"Well done, Harriet," whispered Aunt Formica as she took the rope from me. "Now for some fun!"

Aunt Formica signaled to Aunt Japonica and Aunt Thessalonika to join us in a huddle.

"Can you howl?" she asked.

"I beg your pardon?" asked Aunt Japonica in a low voice. "I thought you said, 'Can you howl?'"

"I did," said Aunt Formica impatiently. "Well, can you?"

"I can," I said. "I think."

"Good," said Aunt Formica. "Now, I'll count to three. When I reach three, we will all howl like coyotes who had something un-pleasant to eat and all have a stomachache. Do you understand?"

"Yes," I said. I had heard coyotes howl in a cowgirl film once, and I knew roughly what they sounded like.

"One," began Aunt Formica. "Two. Three!"

When she reached three, we all lifted our chins, fixed our eyes on the moon, and howled like sick coyotes. It was a terrible, frightening noise.

As the ghostly sound rang out through the darkness, I glanced toward the rustlers. The one who was singing had dropped his guitar, and all the others had dropped their spoons and plates. One was so frightened that he had swallowed his beans the wrong way and one was stuck in his nose. They were clearly terrified.

"Carry on," encouraged Aunt Formica as we paused to get our breath back. "It's working just as I thought it would."

When the second howl came, which was much longer and much more frightening than the first, all five rustlers sprang to their feet and hugged one another for safety, their knees knocking with fright in their blue jeans.

Aunt Formica now stood up. Picking up her rope, she knotted the end into a noose and began to swing it around her head. Wider and wider it went, a perfect lasso, and then, with a final flick of her arm, she sent it snaking out toward the terrified rustlers.

I could hardly believe what I saw, but it really happened. Gently and gracefully, the noose of the lasso settled down around the five huddled rustlers, to be pulled tight by Aunt Formica with one or two deft twists of her wrists. The rustlers were absolutely trapped, their arms pinned to their sides by the lasso.

They could go nowhere and do nothing. They were completely at Aunt Formica's mercy.

We all got up and walked over toward the campfire. As we did so, Aunt Formica gave a sudden tug on the rope, and all the rustlers fell to the ground in a helpless heap. Then,

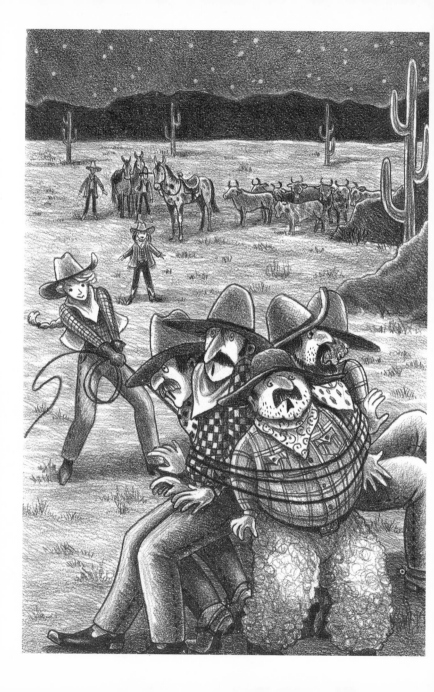

when she reached them and was standing over them, she gave the rope a few further twists to make absolutely sure that they were secured.

Of course, they hardly had time to realize what had happened to them.

"Let us go!" said the biggest of them. "You've got no right to lasso us like that."

Aunt Formica just laughed. "Oh really?" she said. "And did you have any right to steal all my cattle and my horses?"

Of course, the rustlers had no answer to that, and so they stayed exactly where they were, tied up on the ground, while my aunts and I retrieved our tents from the saddle-bags of our horses and pitched them next to the fire.

"Goodnight," called out Aunt Formica to the rustlers. "I hope you won't be too uncomfortable sleeping out there on the hard ground, but then you should have thought of that before you took up rustling!"

And with that remark ringing in everybody's ears, we all went to sleep. I was afraid that I might dream of rattlesnakes, but I didn't. Instead, I had very pleasant, funny dreams about helpful coyotes, and aunts, and other subjects like that.

The next morning, the rustlers all looked very uncomfortable and angry. We mounted our horses, rounded up the cattle, and then came back to the camp to pick up the rustlers. They tried to run away, of course, but they couldn't really get anywhere and just made fools of themselves, stumbling and falling over their feet.

We rode home in comfort, with the poor old rustlers walking tamely behind us. It took a long time to reach the ranch, but at last we got there and dismounted. The rustlers were even more tired than we were and I felt sorry for them. I fetched them some cold water from the house and gave each of them a good drink, which seemed to make them a little bit happier.

"I'm sorry," said the head rustler. "I realize that what we've been doing was very, very wrong."

Aunt Formica looked at him sharply. "It's one thing for you to say that now," she said. "But how can we believe you?"

"I promise," said the rustler. "I cross my heart. Boy Scout's honor."

"Were you ever a Boy Scout?" asked Aunt Formica sternly.

The head rustler hung his head in shame.

"Yes," he mumbled. "I was. That was before I started rustling."

"You should be thoroughly ashamed of yourself," said Aunt Formica. "A Boy Scout becoming a rustler! It's shocking!"

The head rustler looked so embarrassed that I thought he was going to cry.

"I should hand you over to the sheriff," went on Aunt Formica. "But I know that he's not much good. I don't think he's ever dealt with a rustler."

She paused. "What do you think, Harriet?" she asked me. "Do you think we should give them a chance?"

I did not hesitate with my reply. You should always be generous to people once they've learned their lesson, and I was sure that these rustlers had learned theirs.

"Yes," I said. "I think they should get one last chance."

Aunt Formica nodded.

"Very well," she said. "I'll let you go. But you'll have to clean the house first. It's been years since it's had a good spring cleaning, and that's your punishment. Do you understand?"

The rustlers all said yes together. So Aunt Formica untied them and they all trooped off into the house, where they were given brooms and aprons and buckets of water.

They scrubbed and polished and swept. Then they polished again and rubbed and checked to see that every surface was free of dust (and tumbleweed). Then, when they said they had finished, Aunt Formica checked their work and made them do it all over again. They did not complain, though. They had learned their lesson, and they had all decided that they actually liked honest work.

• • •

We stayed with Aunt Formica for five more days. During that time we had so much fun. Aunt Formica taught me all about being a cowgirl. She showed me how to use a lasso and how to shoot a bottle cap off a bottle with my eyes half closed. I also learned to ride well, and by the last day I could stand up in the saddle and jump up and down twice, all at a gallop.

At last we had to leave. I was very sorry to go, as I had enjoyed myself immensely in America and I looked forward to coming back one day. We all rode into Skeleton Gulch, with our suitcases on the backs of the horses. We were a little early for the train, so Aunt Formica suggested that we stop in at the local store where she had things to buy.

The store was a wonderful place, smelling of flour, molasses, and things that horses like to eat. I stood there and looked around, marveling at all the things it sold—wrenches, wire, coffee, beans, plugs . . . plugs! I suddenly remembered my promise to my father.

But would they have the special sort of plug he needed? Probably not.

I was wrong. The shopkeeper, an old man in a white apron, had no difficulty finding what I wanted.

"Good plugs, those," he said. "They're mighty useful for those special camping baths somebody's just invented!"

Our shopping done, we went to the station and watched the distant white smoke of the train draw nearer.

"You must come back, Harriet," said Aunt Formica as she waved good-bye. "Once a cowgirl, always a cowgirl!"

As the train pulled out of the station and began its long journey back, I waved and waved from the window until all I could see of Aunt Formica was the top of her large white hat. Then I went back to my seat. A few minutes later, the conductor came around. I gave him my ticket, and he punched it.

That's funny, I thought. I'm sure I've seen that conductor before. Surely he looks a little bit like . . . Yes, you've guessed right. My aunts had enjoyed their vacation, but it was now time for them to get back to their old tricks!

GRAHAM CLARK

A Note on the Author

Alexander McCall Smith has written more than fifty books, including the *New York Times* bestselling No. 1 Ladies' Detective Agency mysteries and The Sunday Philosophy Club series. A professor of medical law at Edinburgh University, he was born in what is now Zimbabwe and taught law at the University of Botswana. He lives in Edinburgh, Scotland. Visit him at www.alexandermccallsmith.com.

A Note on the Illustrator

Laura Rankin is also the illustrator of the picture books *Rabbit Ears, Swan Harbor*, and *The Handmade Alphabet.* She lives in Maine.